Purr and Pounce

Bringing Home a Cat

by Amanda Doering Tourville
illustrated by Andi Carter

Special thanks to our advisers for their expertise:

Sharon Hurley, D.V.M.
New Ulm (Minnesota)
Regional Veterinary Center

Terry Flaherty, Ph.D.
Professor of English
Minnesota State University,
Mankato

PICTURE WINDOW BOOKS
Minneapolis, Minnesota

Editor: Jill Kalz
Designer: Hilary Wacholz
Page Production: Michelle Biedscheid
Art Director: Nathan Gassman
Associate Managing Editor: Christianne Jones
The illustrations in this book were created with mixed media.
Photo Credit: Gina Smith/Shutterstock, 23

Picture Window Books
151 Good Counsel Drive
P.O. Box 669
Mankato, MN 56002-0669
877-845-8392
www.picturewindowbooks.com

Printed in the United States of America.

All books published by Picture Window Books
are manufactured with paper containing at least
10 percent post-consumer waste.

Library of Congress Cataloging-in-Publication Data
Tourville, Amanda Doering, 1980-
Purr and pounce : bringing home a cat /
by Amanda Doering Tourville ; illustrated by
Andi Carter.
p. cm. – (Get a pet)
Includes index.
ISBN 978-1-4048-4856-6 (library binding)
1. Cats—Juvenile literature. I. Carter, Andi,
1976- ill. II. Title.
SF445.7.T68 2009
636.8–dc22   2008006426

Table of Contents

A New Cat

Victor is getting a new cat tonight! What kind of cat will he get? Will it be a kitten or an older cat? Will it want to play all of the time? Will it want to cuddle?

Most Popular Purebred* Cat Breeds
Persian
Maine Coon
Exotic
Siamese
Abyssinian

* The most popular non-purebred cat in the
United States is the domestic shorthair.

5

Choosing a Cat

Victor is getting his cat from a breeder. Many people get cats from a pet store or animal shelter. Victor wants a gentle, quiet cat. Kittens are cuddly, but they are a lot of work. Older cats are already trained, but they may not be good around kids or other pets.

Victor watches all of the cats carefully. He wants to pick a healthy one. A healthy cat is able to run and jump. It looks at the things going on around it. Its eyes are bright and clear. Its fur is shiny and clean.

Victor finds a cat he likes. He names her Lola.

TIP
Long-haired and medium-haired cats need to be brushed every day. If you don't have time to brush your cat every day, choose a short-haired cat.

Coming Home

Victor's new cat is home! But she is a little scared. Everything is new to her. Victor keeps his cat in one room for the first few days. He lets her get used to the smells and sounds of her new home.

After a few days, Victor lets his cat explore other rooms. He makes sure to play with her every day. He checks her toys for loose strings or tears.

TIP
Cats are crazy about a plant called catnip. The smell of it can make cats act funny. You can get cat toys filled with catnip at your local pet store.

Time to Eat

Victor feeds his cat special cat food he buys at a pet store. It is made from chicken. It includes vitamins his cat needs. Victor also makes sure his cat always has fresh water.

While most of their diet is meat, cats like greens, too. Victor's cat isn't allowed outside, so she can't eat grass. Sometimes, she tries to eat the house plants, instead! This can be very dangerous. To keep his cat happy and healthy, Victor buys cat grass for her to nibble on. Most pet stores sell cat grass.

TIP
Cats like treats. It's OK to give your cat a small number of cat treats. But don't give her human food. It might make her sick.

Grooming

Cats are very clean animals. They spend a lot of time grooming themselves. By licking their fur, cats get rid of dirt and loose hair.

TIP
Brushing your cat can help prevent a hairball. When cats groom themselves, they swallow lots of hair. Sometimes this hair forms a ball in the cat's stomach. The cat then has to cough up the ball.

Victor helps his cat keep her fur clean by brushing her every day. He buys soft grooming brushes at a pet store.

Keeping Clean

Most cats are trained to go to the bathroom in a litter box. By keeping his cat's litter box clean, Victor helps keep his cat healthy.

Victor cleans the waste out of his cat's litter box at least once a day. He begins by scooping out the dirty litter. Then he pours in new litter to take its place. About once a week, Victor throws out all of the litter and cleans the box. He scrubs the box with a wet cloth and soap. He lets the box dry before putting in fresh litter.

TIP

If your cat goes to the bathroom in the wrong place, don't yell at her. After she has eaten, pick her up and put her in the litter box. If she keeps going to the bathroom in the wrong place, she may be sick or unhappy.

Staying Healthy

Cats need to go to the doctor just like people do. Victor takes his cat to the veterinarian for a checkup soon after he gets her. The vet answers Victor's questions. She gives Victor's cat a few shots to keep her healthy.

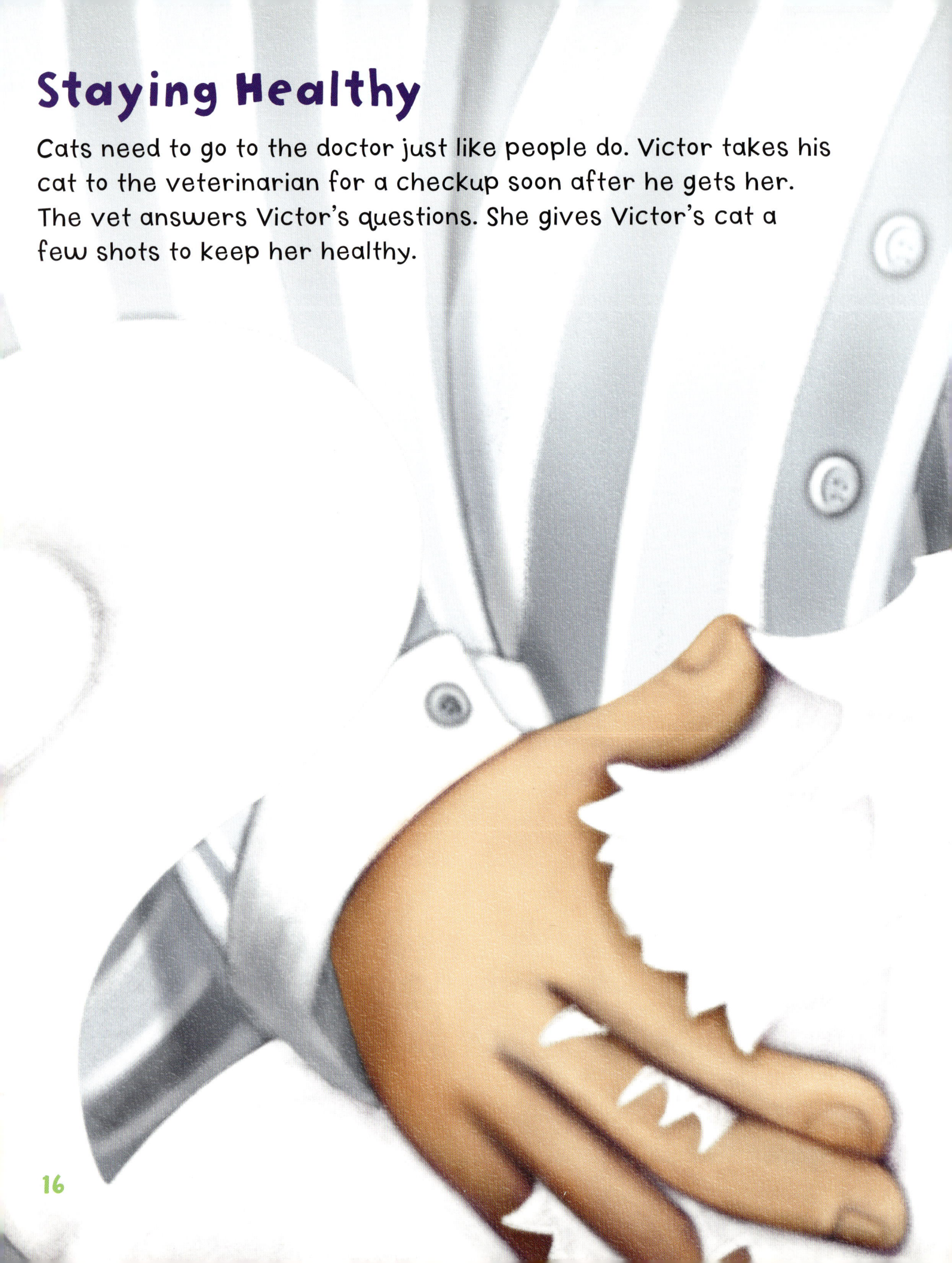

Once a week, Victor gives his cat a checkup at home. He checks her fur for hairless patches or fleas. He feels all over her body for lumps or cuts. A cat's eyes and ears should be clean, her teeth white, and her gums pink. If something doesn't look or feel right, Victor takes his cat to the vet.

TIP
Cats can get sick. If your cat has a runny nose, or is coughing or sneezing a lot, she might be sick. Take her to the vet right away.

Good Night, Kitty!

Victor gets about eight hours of sleep a day. His cat gets twice that much! Cats take "cat naps" throughout the day and night. Although Victor's cat sleeps in many places in the house, she has her own bed, too. It's in a quiet place where she won't be bothered.

Victor never wakes his cat suddenly or picks her up while she is sleeping. She may be surprised and try to bite or scratch him.

TIP
Your cat might make noises or shake in her sleep. Don't worry about her or wake her up. She might be dreaming.

A Happy Pet

Caring for a cat is a lot of work. But it's worth it! Cats are playful, fun to watch, and wonderful to cuddle with. With good care, Victor will have a great furry friend for many years.

Cat Close-up

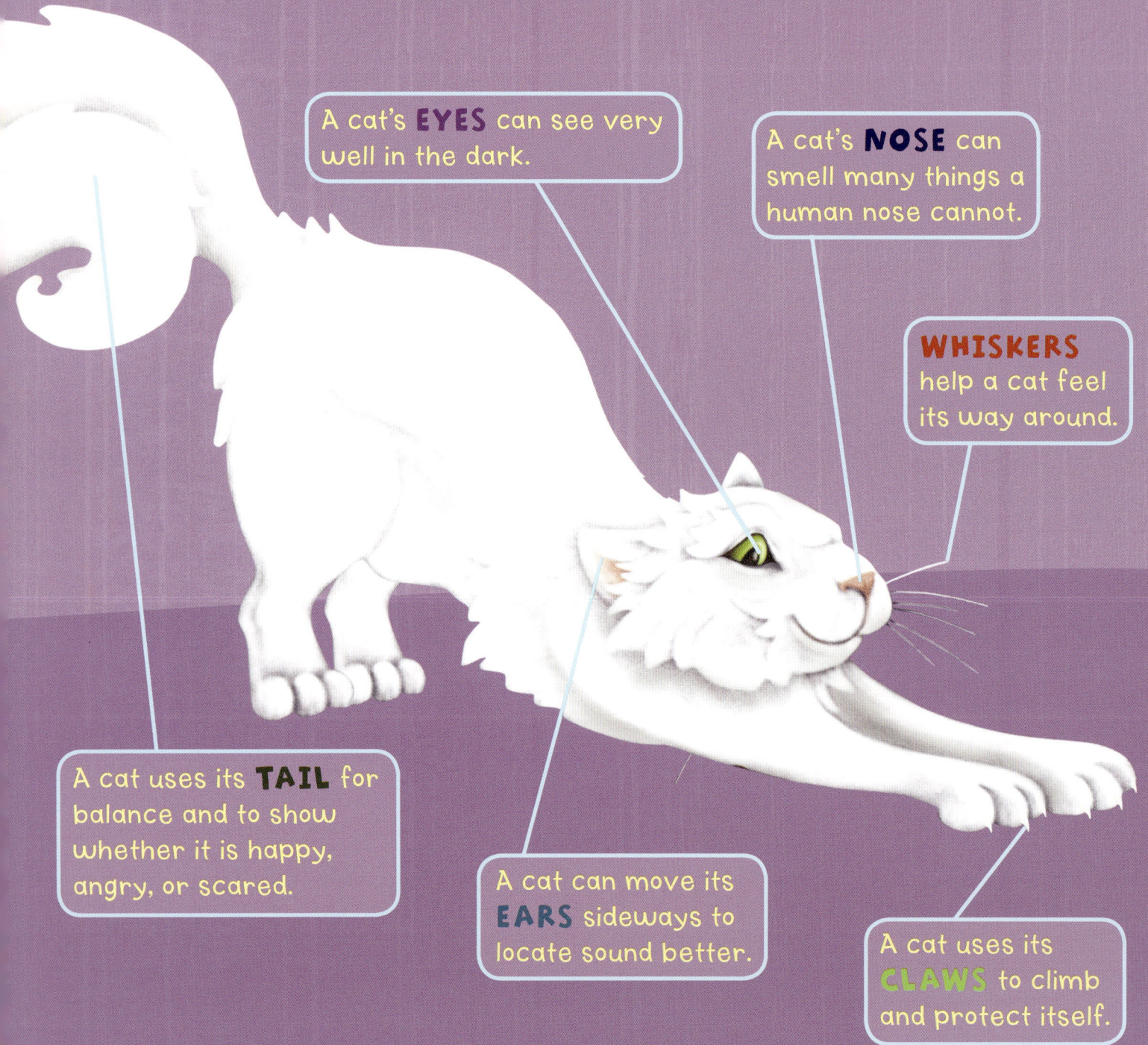

A cat's **EYES** can see very well in the dark.

A cat's **NOSE** can smell many things a human nose cannot.

WHISKERS help a cat feel its way around.

A cat uses its **TAIL** for balance and to show whether it is happy, angry, or scared.

A cat can move its **EARS** sideways to locate sound better.

A cat uses its **CLAWS** to climb and protect itself.

Cat Life Cycle

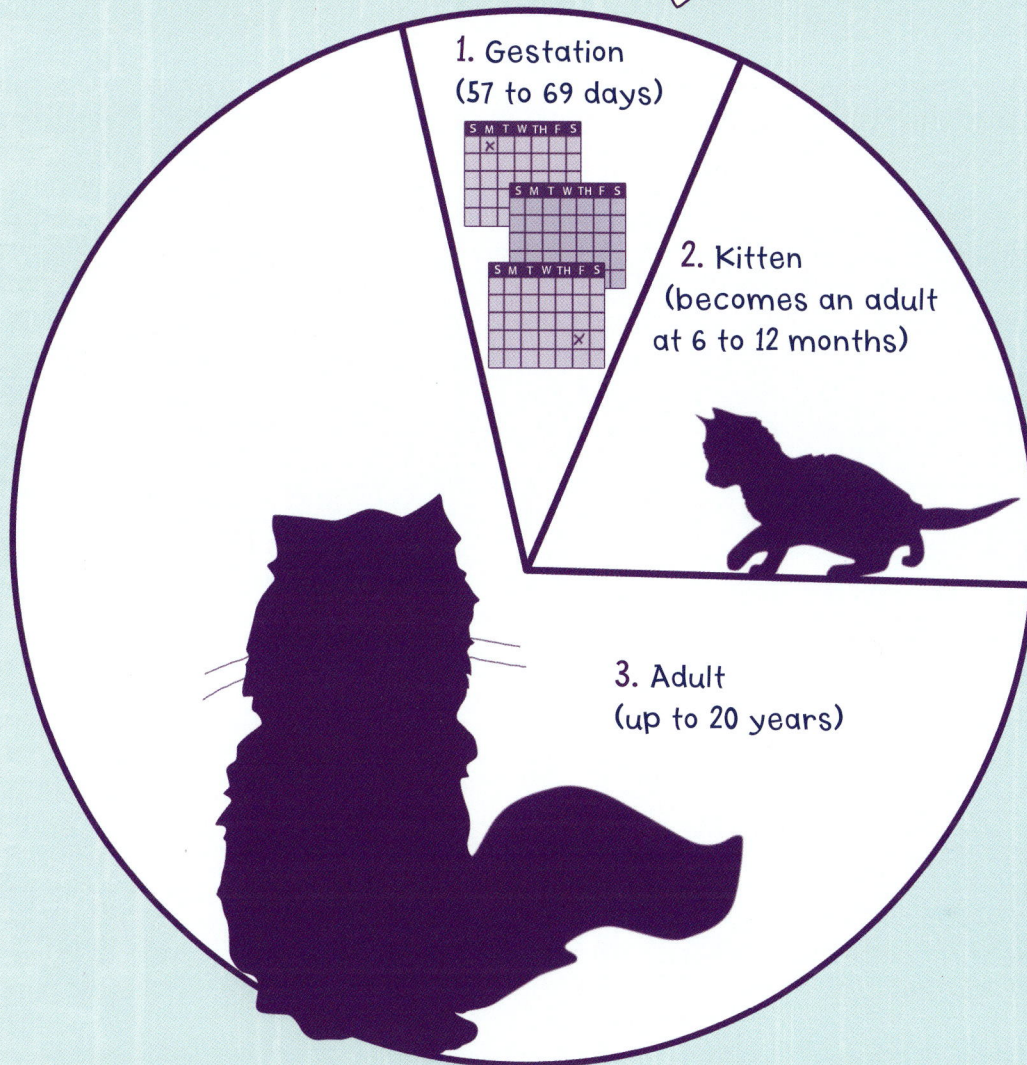

1. Gestation (57 to 69 days)

2. Kitten (becomes an adult at 6 to 12 months)

3. Adult (up to 20 years)

Glossary

animal shelter—a safe place where lost or homeless pets can stay

breed—a kind or type

breeder—a person who raises animals to sell

fleas—tiny bloodsucking insects

gestation—the amount of time an unborn animal spends inside its mother

grooming—cleaning and making an animal look neat

litter—a material that draws in an animal's waste

purebred—having parents of the same breed

veterinarian—a doctor who takes care of animals; vet, for short

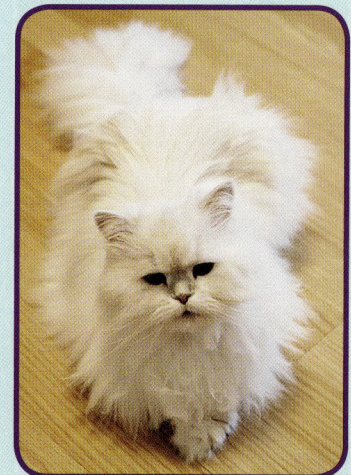

Persian Cat

23

To Learn More

More Books to Read

Dennis-Bryan, Kim. *Kitten Care: A Guide to Loving and Nurturing Your Pet.* New York: DK Pub., 2004.

Hibbert, Clare. *Cat.* North Mankato, Minn.: Smart Apple Media, 2005.

Landau, Elaine. *Your Pet Cat.* New York: Children's Press, 2007.

Walker, Niki, and Bobbie Kalman. *Kittens.* New York: Crabtree Pub. Co., 2004.

On the Web

FactHound offers a safe, fun way to find Web sites related to topics in this book. All of the sites on FactHound have been researched by our staff.

1. Visit *www.facthound.com*
2. Type in this special code: 1404848568
3. Click on the FETCH IT button.

Your trusty FactHound will fetch the best sites for you!

Index

Look for all of the books in the Get a Pet series:

Flutter and Float: Bringing Home Goldfish
Purr and Pounce: Bringing Home a Cat
Scurry and Squeak: Bringing Home a Guinea Pig
Skitter and Scoot: Bringing Home a Hamster
Twitter and Tweet: Bringing Home a Bird
Woof and Wag: Bringing Home a Dog